The SERVANT of TWO MASTERS

By Lance Davis

Based on
"il Servitore di due padroni"

By CARLO GOLDONI

As presented by the Parson's Nose Theater
www.parsonsnose.com

"No man can serve two masters!" – Matthew 6:24

All performing rights reserved
Contact Lance Davis
lance@parsonsnose.com

About Parson's Nose Theater

My wife, actress/director Mary Chalon and I founded Parson's Nose Theater in May, 2000 to help revitalize the classics. To date, our company of professionals, with credits from On and Off Broadway, film and television, has presented over 60 works by the great writers of Western Culture to thousands of Los Angelenos.

Our mission is to present these great works, not only by Shakespeare but Molière, Goldoni, Belasco, Grimm, Chekhov, Perrault and others, in original, "short form" (under 90 minute) adaptations that capture the characters, language, plots, and, most importantly, the spirit of the original authors. We don't do hip-hop or rock and roll, leaving that to better qualified companies. We also don't do stuffy, overly-reverential interpretations.

The spirit we strive to achieve is that of Molière's 17th Century touring company, inspired by the immensely popular Italian comedians of the "commedia dell arte", who celebrated the "live" in "live theater". At PNT we believe that in order to drag audiences away from their screens, theater must once again reinvent itself, breathing new life into our classic works in intimate, newly imagined productions.

Our theater is in an historic, Marston-Van Pelt designed funeral parlor chapel, two blocks from Pasadena City Hall. Our work is intimate, social, and devoted to performing with humor, skill and warmth, inviting our audiences to the "Parson's Nose Experience". As someone described us, "They don't take themselves too seriously, but they take their work very seriously."

I must thank Lewis and Terry Perl, Eileen Davis, and Doctor Mario and Therese Molina for their generous support of our work, and the Parson's Nose Company of exceptional artists who bring such fun to this beloved and unique art form. Most especially, I thank Mary and Jemma.

Goldoni and Molière

Some fascinating things to me, as I look at the lives of Jean Baptiste Poquelin (aka Molière 1622-1673) and Carlo Goldoni (1707-1793) are the small coincidences in their lives, almost one hundred years apart. Goldoni was a huge admirer of Moliere's. "Good, but not yet Molière" was his self-critique. Each was born to an artisan father, though Goldoni later claimed otherwise. Poquelin's mother died when he was a boy, and to relieve the pain his grandfather would take him to see the outlandish street performers on the bridges of the Seine. Goldoni also claimed that his grandfather took him to the theater, though in reality his grandfather died before he was born.

Both trained as lawyers, but both turned their backs on a secure profession to follow their passion for the theater. Goldoni's fascination began while playing with his puppets rather than attend school. Poquelin's journey began when he met the captivating actress Madeleine Bejart, changed his name, and joined her father's theater company, Le Theatre Illustre, later La Troupe de Molière, and played throughout the French provinces for seventeen years.

Both were greatly influenced by the extremely popular and irreverent Italian actors who toured from town to town with their broad, improvisational comedies. Both used this "street comedy" as the basis for their own work, anchoring its plots and characters to a more sophisticated structure while remaining true to its essence of its farcical chaos.

Interestingly, both men's initial writings were hampered by the critical opinion that comedy was artistically inferior to tragedy. Luckily for us, their failed attempts at serious drama, though surely upsetting to them on a personal level, guided them to their true mission - to create comedy, based on human frailty, that would make the whole world laugh.

Their brilliance established the modern comedy of today, from vaudeville to sitcom. Old men, young lovers and wily servants. (Norman Lear?) And if the artist's mission is to create joy and beauty in this world, both succeeded magnificently, and we are the beneficiaries.

CHARACTERS
Smeraldina (Smer-all-DEE-nah), servant to Clarice
Pantalone (Pant-ah-LOW-nay), father to Clarice
Doctor Lombardi (Lom-BAR-di), father to Silvio
Brighella (Brig-AY-la), an innkeeper
Clarice (Clah-REE-chay), in love with Silvio
Silvio (SILL-ve-yo), in love with Clarice
Beatrice (Bee-ah-TREE-chay) also Federigo (Fed-ah-REE-go), in love with Florindo
Florindo (Floor-IN-do), in love with Beatrice, heavy Castillian lisp, at times almost incomprehenthible
Truffaldino, (Truffle-DEE-no) a poor servant

SCENE 1

Throughout, think "a celebration of the spirit of commedia dell arte". Not masks and diamond checks, necessarily, but improvisation, creating "lazzi" ("business"). Try playing with Italian accents at times. Perhaps Florindo is Castillian and we all have to work to understand him.

Pre-show, while audience enters, perhaps very serious, therefore comic butchering of a famous aria or in Commedia gibberish -"grammelot"- or "Bella Notte" from "Lady and the Tramp". Perhaps comic seating manipulation ala Cirque du Soleil, with the usher reading tickets and rearranging patrons as they come in.

Stage: An open stage with a traditional commedia drop (or parachute silk?) of the Port of Venezia. "Brighella's Trattoria" with cafe table in front. Brighella's bad art, perhaps Keane paintings, hanging up for sale.

Note: All seeming violence in the play is done ala Parson's Nose, with "slapsticks" or "pepperonis" – which are four foot pool noodles painted red. Harmless, but make a loud sound.

A sign runs by: "Venezia, Italy - 1750?"

Smeraldina, an adorable peasant maid, sneaks out to talk to audience. She signals music to stop.

SMERALDINA
Ciao. Okay, we're about to start so I'll be quick. Just to clear something up. This play is all supposed to be "improvised", which means we make it all up on the spot, but really a lot of it is written down by Signore Goldoni. And I just want to say that according to him, I, Smeraldina Ronzoni de Pontevecchio, am some kind of a gaga, man-crazy flirt and that is absolutely not true. Hi. What's your name? Are you married? To her? Where was I? So, just to be clear, I am no different from any other female servant of 1750. I work hard to take care of my mistress. If I dream occasionally about a gorgeous guy sweeping me off my feet I'm just like a million other girls trying to make it through, okay? (Off stage: "Smeraldina!") Gotta go. (gestures "call me")

Smeraldina exits. Lights fade, then up.

MUSIC: Festive with trumpets. Vivaldi? Played badly?

Lights up. PANTALONE and his daughter, CLARICE pose for an "engagement" sketch with DR. LOMBARDI and his son SILVIO. BRIGHELLA, with sketch pad. Clarice's servant, SMERALDINA, crashes.

PANTALONE
Come, Doctor Lombardi. Next to me, my friend. You there, Clarice. No, there. And you there, Silvio; not there, there next to your father. Smeraldina...

CLARICE
Next to me. Please, Papa. There. No, there.

PANTALONE
Now then, Brighella. When you're ready.

BRIGHELLA
Say "ricotta"...

He sketches furiously. He finishes.

BrIGHELLA
And...thank you!

LOMBARDI
Wonderful. I'll want a copy. Now then, Silvio...

SILVIO
Si, Papa. (on one knee) Mi Clarice. I know we've had our ups and downs. I haven't always paid as much attention to you as I should. And then you were betrothed and all. But now it looks as though things might have worked out for me, with this Federigo Rasponi dying and all. (I'm getting there, Papa!) And so now I want to ask you...I want to say that if you...Clarice...if you would be my wife, I'd...I'd really appreciate it.

CLARICE
You'd "appreciate" it? Oh yes, Silvio. Yes, I will.

SILVIO
Gosh. That's so great. Wow. She said yes, Papa.

He hugs his father. Then he and Clarice hug. Everybody hugs. Smeraldina hugs Silvio repeatedly.

BRIGHELLA
Everybody hold, please! (They freeze.) Got it!

SILVIO
Oh ti amo, Clarice.

CLARICE
Oh ti amo too, Silvio. I love you so much!

SILVIO
Yeah, but I love you so much more.

CLARICE
No, Silvio, no, I think I love you more…

SILVIO
Oh I think I do.

CLARICE
Seriously…

Smeraldina throws confetti. Pantalone hits a desk bell at Brighella's.

PANTALONE
Heh heh. No "I do's" until the wedding, eh, kids?

SMERALDINA
This isn't the wedding?

PANTALONE
Of course not. They're just engaged.

SMERALDINA
Oh. Then I'll save this…(picking up confetti)

They exit. Brighella brings out a platter. The men munch.

PANTALONE
Ah, Dottore Lombardi, mio buon amico. I am delighted this union between our houses worked out so beautifully. All Venezia will rejoice.

LOMBARDI
Si, si. But Signore Pantalone, I must say I was shocked when I heard that your dowry – I mean your daughter -- was available. I thought Clarice was absolutely spoken for. What happened?

PANTALONE
Ah, Lombardi, it is a tragic story. Si, as everyone knows, Clarice was betrothed to Signor Federigo Rasponi, the great fish merchant of Torino…

LOMBARDI
Yes. Federigo Rasponi. The great fish merchant of Torino.

PANTALONE
Oh, my friend, don't ask me about it. I - I can hardly speak of it.

LOMBARDI
But I must know. Tell me. What happened, Signore?

PANTALONE
He was killed, Lombardi. Morto. In a duello.

LOMBARDI
A duello? Over what?

PANTALONE
Something about his sister. That's all I know. Oh!

LOMBARDI
There, there. Did she love him?

PANTALONE
His sister? Well, I should think so. It's his sister...

LOMBARDI
No, no. Clarice. Your dowry. Did Clarice love him?

PANTALONE
Oh her. She never met him. But, Lombardi, you will understand. He was so - so - very -rich! (weeps)

LOMBARDI
Oh! Oh! (Weeping) Really, really rich then?

PANTALONE
Really, really, really rich...

Both weep uncontrollably.

LOMBARDI
I am so sorry for you, mi amico.

PANTALONE
Oh no. Don't get me wrong. Clarice is most fortunate to have Silvio as a backup.

LOMBARDI
Backup, sure. And her dowry, Signore. It remains the same I assume?

PANTALONE
Of course, Dottore Lombardi. The same. We cannot live on what might have been. Now they must settle for love.

LOMBARDI
Are you going to eat the rest of that?

PANTALONE
No, go ahead.

They weep again. Brighella joins them.

BRIGHELLA
Signori? For whom do we weep?

LOMBARDI
Signore Federigo Rasponi of Torino, Brighella! One of the best...well... richest men who ever lived!

BRIGHELLA
No! Signore Federigo Rasponi of Torino is dead?!

PANTALONE
You knew him, Brighella?

BRIGHELLA
Si, si. When I was a boy in Torino Signore Federigo was the town bully. I was friends with his little sister, Beatrice. Ah, Beatrice. A beautiful girl, but... different.

PANTALONE
How "different", Brighella?

BRIGHELLA
She dressed like a man.

PANTALONE
Ah. Well, "when in Torino", eh?

BRIGHELLA
But that was years ago. Oh this is awful. "Arrivederci, Signore Federigo".

Young people re-enter.

Sounds of Italian arguing, "grammelot" off stage. TRUFFALDINO enters. During next he alternates greeting with shouting to offstage.

TRUFFALDINO
Bon giorno! (calls back "Arrezzipasta bonorosa! Fugellayou!") Bon giorno, Signore. (sees Clarice) Oh! Guarda la ragazza!

PANTALONE
Sirrah! That is my daughter!

TRUFFALDINO
Pardone, Signore. A little humor. Now I see the resemblance. (to Silvio) And look at you! You're a big one!

LOMBARDI
That is my son, sciocco!

TRUFFALDINO
You have children? Science is wonderful. (to Smeraldina) And where did you come from?

SMERALDINA
I'm my mistress' mistress.

PANTALONE
But who are you, sirrah? And where did you come from?

TRUFFALDINO
Excellent questions, Signore! I am Truffaldino Battochio! Born in Bergamo! But my new master - since this morning - comes from the great city of Torino!

PANTALONE
Ah. And what is your master's name?

TRUFFALDINO
His name? Signore Federigo Rasponi!

ALL
Signore Federigo Rasponi?

TRUFFALDINO
Signore Federigo Rasponi!

PANTALONE
Of Torino?

TRUFFALDINO
Of Torino!

ALL
Of Torino?

TRUFFALDINO
Is there an echo? And he is on his way --

ALL
He is on his way...?

TRUFFALDINO
Stop that.

PANTALONE
Impossible, my friend. Federigo Rasponi is dead!

TRUFFALDINO
No, he just looks -- What? He's dead? No!

PANTALONE
Si!

TRUFFALDINO
But when did this happen? Oh this is terrible. This is my first job! I cannot believe this thing. I must see for myself. "Until I put my finger into his side..." I shall return.

He exits.

SILVIO
Papa! I'm frightened. Rasponi is dead, no?

CLARICE
Papa! What will we do if--

SILVIO
You are mine now, Clarice. I will never let you go.

LOMBARDI
Signore Pantalone, Federigo Rasponi is dead. You are certain.

PANTALONE
I saw the letter. There can be no doubt.

Truffaldino enters, outraged.

TRUFFALDINO
Signori! Per vergogna! This is the way Venetians treat a visitor? I am not so much the fool as I look. My master is very alive and well! Ecco!

BEATRICE RASPONI enters dramatically, disguised as her brother, **FEDERIGO**.

BEATRICE
Signore Pantalone di Venezia? Allow me to present myself. Signor Federigo Rasponi de Torino. (grand bow)

PANTALONE
Are you really Federigo Rasponi?

TRUFFALDINO
Of course he is! Are you Venetians blind?

PANTALONE
B-But we heard – but your sister – died in a duel!

BEATRICE
My sister died in a duel? Aha. No, Signore. I was in a duel. For my sister's honor. But I only fell into the River Po.

LOMBARDI
But how do we know that? We-- we need proof!

TRUFFALDINO
Proof? Proof of what?

LOMBARDI
That Federigo Rasponi is alive.

TRUFFALDINO
Proof that he's alive? Well, let me tell you, Pops. I don't know what you do in Venezia, but back in Torino, if a guy's standin' there, lookin' at ya, we assume he's alive. We kinda trust each other that way.

BEATRICE
No, I understand their difficulty. Here are two letters to confirm who I am.

PANTALONE
(reading) It's...true.

LOMBARDI
It's true!

CLARICE
Oh, Silvio! What will we do?

SILVIO
Wait! Brighella, didn't you say you knew Federigo Rasponi?

BRIGHELLA
Si, Signore.

SILVIO
Well?

BRIGHELLA
Out of my way. Let me look.

BEATRICE
(winks) Don't give me away, Brighella. I'll explain later.

BRIGHELLA
(winks) Signore! Welcome to Venezia! Please do me the honor of staying at my humble inn.

BEATRICE
Of course, my old friend!

PANTALONE
Well then. I guess I must welcome you, Signore Federigo.

CLARICE
Oh no, Papa!

PANTALONE
This is my daughter Clarice, Signore.

BEATRICE
Bellissima!

LOMBARDI
And this is my son.

SILVIO
(indignant) I am Silvio Lombardi di Venezia, Signore! And the betrothed of fair Clarice Pantalone di Venezia!

BEATRICE
I beg your pardon? Betrothed, did you say?

PANTALONE
Allow me to explain, Signore. You must understand, we had received news of your death. Perhaps in a bit too much haste, I allowed my daughter and this young man to become engaged. But now, Doctor Lombardi, you see what I must, for honor, do. My daughter is yours, Signore Federigo.

CLARICE
Oh Papa! Nooooooooo!

SILVIO
No, Signore Pantalone! She is mine! I was here first! You! You will answer to me, Rasponi! A duello!

BEATRICE
A duel, sirrah?

SILVIO
I await your choice of weapons.

CLARICE
No! This is awful! (exits. Smeraldina follows)

SILVIO
If this were Puccini I would sing a very passionate song here, but I must seek my beloved. Oh, oh mi Clarice!

He exits.

PANTALONE
Excuse such passion, Signore. They're very young.

BEATRICE
In time she will come to her senses and realize how good a husband I will be. But now, to more serious matters. The dowry.

PANTALONE
The dowry. Of course. I will have the papers drawn up for us to sign.

BEATRICE
Multo bene, Signore Pantalone. I will be at Brighella's. And oh, I'm afraid I brought little cash with me, for fear of highwaymen. I must ask an advance on my dowry?

PANTALONE
Oh. Well. But of course.

BEATRICE
I will send my servant for it.

PANTALONE
Your servant?

Truffaldino waves.

PANTALONE
Si.

Smeraldina enters.

SMERALDINA
Signore Pantalone? Could you come? Clarice wants to scream at you.

PANTALONE
Si. I'm coming. (Ear plugs) See? I'm coming.

He exits.

BEATRICE
Now then, what's next, my man?

TRUFFALDINO
Next? Lunch, perhaps, Signore? There's a special at the aquarium?

BEATRICE
No, I'm not hungry. I'll eat later. Go. Wait for me.

TRUFFALDINO
Where?

BEATRICE
Where I'm not.

TRUFFALDINO
It's not fair. I could eat a -- (SFX cat sound O.S.) No. It would be wrong...

Truffaldino exits. (SFX: worried cat)

BRIGHELLA
Signora Beatrice, what have you gotten yourself into?

BEATRICE
Oh, Brighella. I've been living by my wits for days now. You know that Federigo is dead.

BRIGHELLA
I'm so sorry.

BEATRICE
Don't be. He was a brute.

BRIGHELLA
Yes he was. How did you kill him?

BEATRICE
I didn't kill him, Brighella. You remember I've always been in love with that brilliant but starving tango teacher, Florindo Aretusi!

BRIGHELLA
Ah yes, Florindo!

BEATRICE
We were to be married. But Federigo refused to allow it because he would have to pay Florindo my dowry. So he challenged Florindo to a duel!

BRIGHELLA
A duel! What happened?

BEATRICE
Florindo won. Federigo lost.

BRIGHELLA
Lost?

BEATRICE
Morto. They were by the River Po at dawn. It was foggy. He rushed at Florindo. Florindo bent to buckle his shoe. Right into the Po. Florindo fled to Venezia. I have followed him here.

BRIGHELLA
But why this disguise, Signora?

BEATRICE
Partly because I like it. It's slimming. But mostly because I need the dowry Pantalone owed Federigo for his marriage to Clarice. I shall use it to find my Florindo. We shall go to America! And open a dance studio in Brooklyn!

BRIGHELLA
With Federigo.

BEATRICE
Florindo. Federigo's dead. I'm Federigo.

BRIGHELLA
But why don't you just tell Signore Pantalone you're your brother's legal heir and then he would have to --

BEATRICE
Brighella. I am but a woman. By the ancient Venetian "Law of Calzone" Signore Pantalone could become my guardian, own my inheritance, and put me in a convent.

BRIGHELLA
And he would. He's a big provolone around here.

BEATRICE
It's just until I find Florindo. Oh pray God he is truly in Venezia. Won't you help me? Please, Brighella?

BRIGHELLA
Of course! You have my word…Signore Federigo!

BEATRICE
Multi grazie!

They exit.

SCENE 2

Truffaldino enters, speaks to audience. His stomach groans. (music SFX?)

TRUFFALDINO
"I'll eat later." (groan) Don't groan at me! I hear you! Did they eat anything in that last scene? They did, didn't they? (groan) I bet they had hoagies. Did they have hoagies? (groan) (goes into audience, begging) Did anybody bring anything to eat? What's in that bag? Oh I can't go on like this. I must say, my new master is terrible. I just may be forced to take my services elsewhere.

SFX (O.S) A dropped trunk. A scream.

FLORINDO (O.S.)
Imbeccille! You drop the luggage! Did not I tell you not to drop the luggage?! You do exactly the oppothite thing; you drop the luggage. Take that! (Smack)

Florindo enters.

FLORINDO
It is thuch a bother. Now I have to find another thervant!

TRUFFALDINO
Bongiorno, Signore!

FLORINDO
Who are you?

TRUFFALDINO
A poor servant, Signore, carving his way through life.

FLORINDO
A thervant! Do you need emplayment?

TRUFFALDINO
Need what?

FLORINDO
Emplayment?

TRUFFALDINO
I have emplayment. I need a hoagie.

FLORINDO
Perhaps you will work for me, little man?

TRUFFALDINO
Well, perhaps, Signore.

FLORINDO
You are at liberty? You have no mester?

TRUFFALDINO
Mester… master? Now?

FLORINDO
Of curth, now.

TRUFFALDINO
At this moment?

FLORINDO
At this moment.

TRUFFALDINO
Not really.

FLORINDO
Then I, Florindo Aretuthi, will take the chanth with you. You may work for me. Get my bags.

TRUFFALDINO
Si, Signore! Si!

Truffaldino runs off. Sound of luggage. Grammelot argument with former servant. He returns, carrying a wall of luggage.

TRUFFALDINO
Here I am, Signore!

FLORINDO
Where ith my toilette? You forget my toilette.

Truffaldino staggers off, back on with one more tiny bag in his teeth.

FLORINDO
Now then, I need a rum.

TRUFFALDINO
A rum? There's a full bar…

FLORINDO
No, a rum.

TRUFFALDINO
I'm sorry…

FLORINDO
A rum, where I slip.

TRUFFALDINO
"Room"! You need a room! I know just the place, Signore. Here. The owner is a friend. I may be able to arrange it. And look! They have a restaurant. And look! It's lunchtime!

FLORINDO
Later. Right now you must run an errnd.

TRUFFALDINO
A what?

FLORINDO
An ernd. You go…you do the thing... You --

TRUFFALDINO
Oh "errand".

FLORINDO
That's what I said. Ernd.

TRUFFALDINO
Si, Signore.

FLORINDO
Go to the pistal office.

TRUFFALDINO
Postal office...

FLORINDO
Ask if there is any meal...

TRUFFALDINO
Mail...

FLORINDO
...for Florindo Aretusi. Capisci?

TRUFFALDINO
God bless you. And then we eat?

FLORINDO
And then we eat. What is your name, little man?

TRUFFALDINO
Truffaldino Battachio di Bergamo, Signore!

FLORINDO
Exthellent. If you do well, you have a bright future as my thlave!

TRUFFALDINO
Grazie, Signore. And my payment?

FLORINDO
Will be commenthurate. I may even give you a celery.

Florindo exits.

TRUFFALDINO
A "celery"! Wow. Before this I've only been "paid", but a "celery"! Hey, maybe my other master should give me a celery. Wow. Two masters, two celeries! And if one of them would give me money I could buy a hoagie.

Beatrice enters with Brighella.

BEATRICE
You! I thought you were getting my luggage!

TRUFFALDINO
I just did!

BEATRICE
You did?

TRUFFALDINO
Oh. No. Sorry. I'll get it now, Signore.

BEATRICE
Bring it here. I'm staying at Brighella's.

TRUFFALDINO
No.

BEATRICE
I'm not?

TRUFFALDINO
Well, you can...

BEATRICE
Get my luggage. Bring it here. And on your way, stop at the post office and see if there are any messages for me or my sister, Signora Beatrice Rasponi.

BRIGHELLA
(sotto voce) Letters, Signora?

BEATRICE
My steward will write me here until I find Florindo. Truffaldino! My luggage, my letters.

TRUFFALDINO
Then lunch. I fly like the wind, maestro.

Beatrice and Brighella exit.

TRUFFALDINO
Letters, luggage, lunch. I'll get the luggage later. Letters. For Beatrice Rasponi, Florindo Rasponi, and Federigo Aretusi. No. Beatrice Aretusi. Rasponi Federigo...no. All I can think of is the lunch. Federigo Minestrone, Florindo Pannetone and Beatrice Mascarpone.

Silvio enters.

SILVIO
Where is your master, sirrah?

TRUFFALDINO
Signore?

SILVIO
Your master?

TRUFFALDINO
Yes. My master. (aside) Which one? (points to Brighella's) In there.

SILVIO
You must deliver a message.

TRUFFALDINO
Well I'm on a pretty tight schedule…

SILVIO
Tell him that his rival in love awaits him. Sbrigati!

Florindo enters.

FLORINDO
Ah! Truffaluffo!

TRUFFALDINO
That's "Truffaldino". I'm getting your luggage now!

FLORINDO
Who is that man?

TRUFFALDINO
Oh, he wants to see my master.

FLORINDO
I do not know him. Why does he want to thee me?

TRUFFALDINO
He's a Venetian, Signore. A bit pazzo. (gestures "crazy") I'll get your letters.

Truffaldino exits.

FLORINDO
Signore? You wish to see me?

SILVIO
Hm? No. I'm here to see the gutless master of that ninny.

FLORINDO
That ninny is my ninny, Signore!

SILVIO
What? The man I seek is Federigo Rasponi.

FLORINDO
He is dead, Signore. (I hope.)

SILVIO
Dead? Indeed he is not, Signore. This very morning I spoke to him.

FLORINDO
Impothible!

SILVIO
Here he stood just hours ago.

FLORINDO
(aside) Federigo Rathponi here? How can that be? He plopped into the Po! I thought I killed him. I must be thlipping.

SILVIO
Are you all right, Signore?

FLORINDO
Si, si.

SILVIO
Come, let's start over. Your name, sir?

FLORINDO
My name?

SILVIO
This should be easy...

FLORINDO
Orazio Ardenti!

SILVIO
Ah. Silvio Lombardi. A pleasure.

FLORINDO
Grazie.

SILVIO
If I can be of any assistance, please call on me.

FLORINDO
I will, Signore. Grazie.

Silvio exits. Truffaldino enters carrying Beatrice's luggage and letters.

TRUFFALDINO
Here, Signore! The letters, the luggage...

FLORINDO
Quickly, Truffilippo. I must return to Torino. Something has arisen. Do you have a letter for me?

TRUFFALDINO
Si, Signore. (fumbling through letters)

FLORINDO
Well then, give it to me.

TRUFFALDINO
Si, Signore, I just have to--

FLORINDO
(reaching) Is this one?

TRUFFALDINO
Stop that. You are such a greedy-- They're not all for you.

FLORINDO
No? Why not?

TRUFFALDINO
(improvising) Because, you see, as I went to the post office I ran into a friend...another servant...who asked me to pick up his master's letters also. So if I can just -- No, that's not --

FLORINDO
What is your problem, little servant man? Can you not read?

TRUFFALDINO
What? Oh that's right! I can't. That must be it.

FLORINDO
Give me those. (aside) What is thith? This is addrethed to "Beatrice Rasponi"! Little man, your friend. What is hith name?

TRUFFALDINO
Er - Pasquale.

FLORINDO
Pasquale. Do you know his mester?

TRUFFALDINO
I never met him. Can I have the letter?

FLORINDO
No. I must peruthe it. (rips open) "Thignora Beatrice, we know you fled to Venezia to thearch for your lover, disguised as your dead brother. You should know there is a warrant for your own arretht, as Florindo's accomplith in Federigo's death. God go with you, Signora. Your thervant Antonio." I could kith you, Antonio! Beatrice here in Venezia! I must find her. Hola! Puffalino!

TRUFFALDINO
Truffaldino.

FLORINDO
Find Pathquale. Find his mester. And bring him to me.

TRUFFALDINO
He'll want the letter.

FLORINDO
Oh. Here.

TRUFFALDINO
But it's opened, Signore.

FLORINDO
What of that?

TRUFFALDINO
He'll think I opened it.

FLORINDO
Of course not. You can't read. Why would you open it? Hurry, Trampolino!

TRUFFALDINO
And then we leave for Torino?

FLORINDO
No. That will not now be nethethary. Find Pasquale and his mester! Hurry!

Florindo exits.

TRUFFALDINO
What about lunch?! Don't you people like Italian food? And how am I supposed to deliver this now that he's opened it? (goes into audience) Who has gum? Ah! (reaches under chair, chews, seals letter) That should do it!

Beatrice enters.

BEATRICE
Truffaldino, where have you been? Is that my luggage?

TRUFFALDINO
Si, Signore. Your luggage.

BEATRICE
Have you been to the post office?

TRUFFALDINO
Si, Signore. There was a letter for your sister.

BEATRICE
Sirrah! This letter's been opened!

TRUFFALDINO
No. See? It's sealed.

BEATRICE
Sealed with -- (sniff)-- Tutti Frutti?

TRUFFALDINO
Tutti Frutti! The best!

BEATRICE
Has anyone read this letter, sirrah?

TRUFFALDINO
No, Signore!

BEATRICE
You'd better be telling the truth! Now unpack my bags. Then we'll eat. (reads) (aside) Oh thank you, Antonio! (aloud) Have you seen Signore Pantalone?

TRUFFALDINO
No, Signore.

BEATRICE
(aside) I must find him. I need that dowry so we can escape to Brooklyn! Oh Florindo!

Beatrice exits.

TRUFFALDINO
You all heard him! He said we'd eat. And I believe him.

Panatalone enters grasping a bag of money.

PANTALONE
Where is your master?

TRUFFALDINO
In there, Signore. (points)

PANTALONE
Where?

TRUFFALDINO
(aside) Here, right?

PANTALONE
Where?

TRUFFALDINO
No, it was…there.

PANTALONE
Well make up your mind!

TRUFFALDINO
Here. Final answer.

PANTALONE
I have his money.

TRUFFALDINO
Where?

PANTALONE
Here. Stop that. (mops his brow) I want you to -- to take it to him.

TRUFFALDINO
To whom?

PANTALONE
To your master. It's for him. It's time for me…to give it to him.

The following lazzi is the miser trying to let go of his money bag but just can't do it. Finally it's like he's in painful labor, wailing, giving birth, with Truffaldino as midwife.

TRUFFALDINO
I'd be delighted.

PANTALONE
I'm going to give it to you now. Here. It…(he tries, can't let go) Oh God.

TRUFFALDINO
Signore. You can do it.

PANTALONE
No I can't. It's money! I can't. Let. Go…

TRUFFALDINO
You can. Give it…

Pantalone tries again to give it to him. Fails. Exhausted.

PANTALONE
I can't. I can't give you the money.

TRUFFALDINO
You can. Get comfortable. Spread your legs. Think about something else. We'll try again. Look at me. Don't look at the bag. Okay?

PANTALONE
Okay.

TRUFFALDINO
Let's go. Look at me! Keep breathing! Good. Now give me the money.

Pantalone locks his eyes on Truffaldino.

TRUFFALDINO
Breathe. "When you walk through a storm, hold your head up high"…Look at me. Big one. I see the zipper. Big push. "Walk on, walk on. With love in.. " There! You did it! It's beautiful. Yes you are, yes you are. Good for you, sir!

PANTALONE
I did it! All by myself! Oh. Oh I have to rest now. Yes. Yes…

Pantalone waddles off. Florindo enters.

FLORINDO
Tiramithu! Where is Pasquale?

TRUFFALDINO
Who? Pasquale! Haven't been able to find him yet, Signore.

FLORINDO
Well what have you been doing?

TRUFFALDINO
I have your money.

FLORINDO
My money?

TRUFFALDINO
Weren't you expecting money?

FLORINDO
I had arranged for a loan.

In following exchange, "Subliminal" lazzi.

TRUFFALDINO
Well here it is! That's great! (Let's eat.)

FLORINDO
There wasn't a methage?

TRUFFALDINO
A what? No message. Just the money. (Let's eat.) Just "give it to your master".

FLORINDO
And I am your mester...am I not...?(hypnotizing him?)

TRUFFALDINO
Yes...Master... (Gives him the money. Snaps out of it.)

FLORINDO
Now find Pasquale.

TRUFFALDINO
I will sir. (swoons) I'm sorry. It's hard to focus when you're starving.

FLORINDO
You're starving? Why did you not say? We'll eat.

TRUFFALDINO
Fantastico!

FLORINDO
As soon as you find Pasquale.

They exit.

SCENE 3

Clarice and Pantalone. Smeraldina watches them as if a soap opera.

CLARICE
Waaaaaa!

PANTALONE
Now my dear--

CLARICE
Waaaaaa!

PANTALONE
If you'd just consider marrying Signore Federigo...

CLARICE
I want Silvio! Silviosilviosilvio...

PANTALONE
But Federigo is successful. And handsome.

CLARICE
I don't want successful and handsome. I want Silvio!

Beatrice enters, unnoticed.

PANTALONE
Pah! You don't know what you're saying! You're just a girl. Well you've had your chance. I am your father! You'll do as you're told.

CLARICE
I won't!

SMERALDINA
Psst! (points to Beatrice)

BEATRICE
Signore Pantalone?

PANTALONE
Ah! Signore! We were just planning the wedding. Very well, dear. Little sausages it is. Now then, you received the money, Signore?

BEATRICE
Money? Why, no.

PANTALONE
But I gave it to your servant.

BEATRICE
Then he must still have it. I'll get it later. Clarice is still upset?

PANTALONE
You must be patient, Signore. She was so happy when she heard you were dead. And now that you aren't--

BEATRICE
I understand. Let me talk to her.

PANTALONE
Of course. Come away, Smeraldina.

Pantalone and Smeraldina exit.

BEATRICE
Signora Clarice--

CLARICE
You waste your time, Signore. I won't marry you. I don't love you. I hate you.

BEATRICE
But, Signora--

CLARICE
You have nothing to say that could possibly interest me.

BEATRICE
Then you won't hear my secret.

CLARICE
You have a secret? Oh tell me! Oh please!

BEATRICE
You have pledged your heart to another, Clarice? Well -- so have I!

CLARICE
Is -- is this true, Signore?

BEATRICE
I am not Federigo Rasponi. I am -- his sister!

CLARICE
Shut. Up. (Beatrice flashes.) You are! I saw them! Oho! Only a woman could be so clever. But your brother?

BEATRICE
He died.

CLARICE
I'm sorry...

BEATRICE
Don't be. He tried to kill my Florindo in a duel. Florindo fled to Venezia. I followed him in this disguise and I search for him now. We're going to start a dance studio in Brooklyn.

CLARICE
Oh! That is sooo romantic!

BEATRICE
It is, isn't it? So you see? You are safe from me.

CLARICE
Oh grazie, Signore!

BEATRICE
But you must not betray me.

CLARICE
Of course not! Your secret is safe. Wait till I tell Silvio!

BEATRICE
No.

CLARICE
Right.

BEATRICE
Then we are friends?

CLARICE
Eternally!

They embrace. Pantalone enters.

PANTALONE
Now that's more like it! You seem to have a bloom in your cheek, my daughter. You've come to your senses, I see.

CLARICE
Si, father. I will obey you in every thing.

PANTALONE
Excellent.

BEATRICE
I told you I'd bring her round, Signore. (wink to Clarice) Mi gelato! (blows kiss).

CLARICE
Mi cannoli! (blows kiss).

BEATRICE
Mi caramella!

PANTALONE
Hoho! Well, this passion mustn't be stemmed any longer! Very well, bambini. You will be married tomorrow.

CLARICE
Tomorrow?!

BEATRICE
Tomorrow?!

PANTALONE
Tomorrow. I'll tell Silvio. He'll take it like a man.

CLARICE
An angry man.

PANTALONE
Do you think? I'll take a pepperoni just in case. You ready yourselves for your big day!

Pantalone exits.

CLARICE
What do we do now?

BEATRICE
It's worse than before!

Clarice and Beatrice exit.

SCENE 4

Silvio and Lombardi. Silvio paces furiously.

SILVIO
Don't try to stop me, father. He shall keep his word or he shall pay.

LOMBARDI
But, Silvio --

SILVIO
He is despicablissima, Papa!

LOMBARDI
Son--

SILVIO
He is vile!

LOMBARDI
My boy --

SILVIO
He's a double dealing, slimy old man who just happens to be the father of the woman I love.

LOMBARDI
My boy, losing your temper will gain you nothing. You are too young to understand these things. Calmness, civility. That's the ticket. Reasonable discourse will get you much further than childish ranting. Now, go away. I will reason with him, and then I will speak with you.

SILVIO
Well, maybe you're right. Very well, father.

Silvio exits. Pantalone enters.

PANTALONE
Ah, Dottore Lombardi, I was just --

LOMBARDI
(enraged) Pantalone! Bastinado! There! There you are!

PANTALONE
Uh --

LOMBARDI
This is how you treat La Casa di Lombardi?

PANTALONE
I really --

LOMBARDI
Stronzo! Have you no respect?

PANTALONE
I don't --

LOMBARDI
(hand gestures) That's for you! Fa! And that! Fa! And one of these! May you find poop in your pesto for the rest of your days! Remember well the ancient words of the Lombardis: "Gallia est divisa in tres partes!" We will be revenged "ex officio," "ipso facto", and "post partum"! I close the curtain of our friendship for all eternity!

Lombardi leaves in a rage.

PANTALONE
Check that guy for rabies! Yo, Doc! The Rasponis are ten times as wealthy as the Lombardis. And my new son-in-law will inherit the whole thing!

Silvio enters.

SILVIO
Aha!

PANTALONE
Oh great. The fruit of the loon.

SILVIO
I challenge you, Signore.

PANTALONE
You can't challenge me. I'm an old man.

SILVIO
Man? I don't think so. Worm, perhaps...

PANTALONE
Watch your tongue, tight thighs.

SILVIO
You old goat --

Silvio grabs Pantalone's pepperoni.

PANTALONE
You don't frighten me, snot nose!

Beatrice enters.

SILVIO
Aha! Just the man I seek!

PANTALONE
That's what you said to me.

SILVIO
That was practice. (turns) If you'd just stayed dead, Signore, Clarice would be mine. Take that! And that!

Silvio swings pepperoni at Beatrice, who pulls out rubber dagger. Silvio knocks the dagger from her hand. She runs into the audience.

BEATRICE
Help! Quickly! Give me a pepperoni! Oh! Men never have a pepperoni when we need one.

Beatrice reaches under audience seat, pulls out a pepperoni, and leaps onto stage. A ferocious pepperoni fight ensues. Errol Flynn and Basil Rathbone. At last, she disarms him, just as Clarice runs on. Pantalone runs off.

CLARICE
Enough! Signore Federigo!

BEATRICE
Remember your oath, Signora!

Beatrice runs off.

CLARICE
Silvio, are you hurt?

SILVIO
As if you cared!

CLARICE
Silvio! What do you mean?

SILVIO
I mean I heard you. You swore an oath to Federigo?

CLARICE
No! I swore an oath with Federigo!

SILVIO
What was it?

CLARICE
I can't tell you.

Smeraldina enters.

SILVIO
You put a dagger into my heart!

CLARICE
But I love you!

SILVIO
I did love you, Clarice! But now --

CLARICE
Silvio! I couldn't live without your love!

SILVIO
Prove it!

CLARICE
Prove it? You want me to prove my love, Silvio? (picks up dagger, holds it to her heart) See? And whatabout you, Silvio? What are you gonna prove?

SILVIO
You want me to prove my love? Give me that dagger.

CLARICE
Get your own dagger.

SILVIO
Just for a minute. I'll give it back.

Smeraldina steps between them.

SMERALDINA
Stop! Both of you! You're ridiculous! What kind of man would ask his woman to prove herself? What kind of a woman would listen?!

CLARICE
(aloof) I deeply regret, Silvio, that your desire is for my death. Perhaps I shall grant your wish, by dying …The Death of Grief. I leave you now. Now…

Clarice starts off, then corrects her exit and wafts off the other way.

SMERALDINA
Well? What have you got to say?

SILVIO
You think she means it? She'll die the Death of Grief?

SMERALDINA
You're the boyfriend. You tell me. You're just going to sit there? You're not going to stop her?

SILVIO
She betrayed our love.

SMERALDINA
She did not! She's a woman! This is the 18th Century. It's run by men. She's being forced into marriage to a man she doesn't know, by her father, a man who doesn't know her. And you! She only asks you to trust her, and look how you act. Oh, mi bella Signora!

Smeraldina runs off.

SILVIO
(aside) Do you think she's right? Wait a minute. She's a woman herself. Of course she'd take Clarice's side. I will still have my revenge. Federigo!

He dashes off.

SCENE 5

Truffaldino enters.

TRUFFALDINO
Just my luck. Two masters on diets. I hope they don't show up together.

Florindo enters hurriedly.

FLORINDO
Trumpolino --

TRUFFALDINO
Truffaldino.

FLORINDO
Where is Pathquale? (aside) I mutht find my Beatrice.

TRUFFALDINO
You told me to find him after we ate.

FLORINDO
I did?

TRUFFALDINO
You did.

FLORINDO
But I'm not hongry. I shall go to the pistal office myself and thee what I can find out. Here, put this money in my room.

Florindo exits.

TRUFFALDINO
(Aside) Well, he's getting closer to a commitment. But I'm not waiting. I'll put the money in his room and then --

Beatrice enters.

BEATRICE
Truffaldino! Is that my money?

TRUFFALDINO
Your money?

BEATRICE
From Signore Pantalone?

TRUFFALDINO
I... think so.

BEATRICE
You think so? Did Pantalone give it to you?

TRUFFALDINO
Si.

BEATRICE
And what did he say?

TRUFFALDINO
To give it to my master.

BEATRICE
Am I your master?

TRUFFALDINO
Si.

BEATRICE
So?

TRUFFALDINO
Sigh. (hands bag to Beatrice) (aside) What will my other master say? But -- if it's not his, he won't say anything, right?

BEATRICE
Signore Pantalone is joining me for dinner.

TRUFFALDINO
Really?

BEATRICE
I want you to choose the menu.

TRUFFALDINO
You want -- you want me to choose the menu?

BEATRICE
Can you do it?

TRUFFALDINO
It's my life! Signore, you shall have a feast!

BEATRICE
Lunch will do. I'm going to meet him. I want it ready when I get back. And here. Take this. Be extremely careful! It's a Loan Agreement for 40,000 lire.

TRUFFALDINO
40,000 lire!

BEATRICE
I'm giving you a chance to prove yourself, sirrah.

TRUFFALDINO
I shall not disappoint you, Signore!

BEATRICE
See that you don't.

Beatrice exits.

TRUFFALDINO
This is the first time anyone has ever asked me to make the menu. Oh I wish mama -- (goes into audience) Do you have a phone? Could I borrow it? Don't worry, no Roman charges. (phones) Mama? It's me, Mama! I'm in Venezia! It's beautiful. Mama, I just wanted you to know that my new master has asked your Truffaldino to make the menu! Si, Mama. Pretty good, eh? Grazie, Mama. I have to go, I just wanted -- No, I can't talk to Papa. I -- Papa! How are you? I'm in Venezia, Papa. Well I have to go, I can't talk to little -- Paulo? Venezia. I have to go, Paulo. Mama will tell you everything. I'll bring you a toy. A gondola. Ciao, Paulo. (to audience) It's family. Oh, Innkeeper?

Brighella appears.

BRIGHELLA
Truffaldino!

TRUFFALDINO
My good man, my master will be dining here in a few minutes with a very important guest.

BRIGHELLA
Who?

TRUFFALDINO
Signore Pantalone.

BRIGHELLA
Oh.

TRUFFALDINO
May I see your menu?

BRIGHELLA
You can't read.

TRUFFALDINO
No. But I want to see it.

BRIGHELLA
There.

TRUFFALDINO
(glances, hands it back) Very nice. Now then. If we were to dine here, what would you suggest?

BRIGHELLA
A nurse. Kidding. How many dishes, in how many courses?

TRUFFALDINO
Two dishes…in two courses.

BRIGHELLA
We have a special. Eight dishes in eight courses.

TRUFFALDINO
Three dishes in four courses.

BRIGHELLA
Six dishes in five courses.

TRUFFALDINO
Four dishes, in three courses.

BRIGHELLA
Done.

TRUFFALDINO
Now then. What would you start with?

BRIGHELLA
Antipasto della Brighella.

TRUFFALDINO
Consisting of --

BRIGHELLA
Cannellini and Spam.

TRUFFALDINO
Excellent. And then?

BRIGHELLA
Then a zuppa. Then a friggin 'do.

TRUFFALDINO
What's a friggin 'do?

BRIGHELLA
Gorgonzola in sheep fat.

TRUFFALDINO
Beautiful. The zuppa?

BRIGHELLA
Squid.

TRUFFALDINO
Excellent. Next?

BRIGHELLA
Rostiti.

TRUFFALDINO
What kind?

BRIGHELLA
Pig brains.

TRUFFALDINO
With a sauce?

BRIGHELLA
We're not barbarians. Kidney Creme.

TRUFFALDINO
For dessert?

BRIGHELLA
A Trifle.

TRUFFALDINO
I think we deserve something more than a trifle!

BRIGHELLA
It's a pudding.

TRUFFALDINO
Anything floating in it?

BRIGHELLA
Not yet.

TRUFFALDINO
Very good. Now then. The table setting. Presentation is everything.

BRIGHELLA
Of course. At Trattoria Brighella we place the food -- on the table.

TRUFFALDINO
Pazzo. We won't just "place the food -- on the table"! "Presentation"!

BRIGHELLA
Very well. We put the antipasta here, zuppa here, rostiti here--

TRUFFALDINO
Wait. Where's the friggin 'do?

BRIGHELLA
Here. Zuppa's there.

TRUFFALDINO
Zuppa's here.

BRIGHELLA
No.

TRUFFALDINO
Stop. Here. (Pulls out loan paper. Tears pieces) Antipasta. Antipasta. (tears) Zuppa.. Zuppa.

BRIGHELLA
Friggin 'do?

TRUFFALDINO
(tearing paper) Here and here.

Beatrice enters with Pantalone.

BEATRICE
Sirrah! What are you doing?

TRUFFALDINO
Dinner.

BEATRICE
My loan! You just shredded 40,000 lire, you --!

Beatrice grabs a pepperoni and pummels Truffaldino into the inn. Brighella stands aside and adds audial.

BRIGHELLA
Ooh! Ah! Oh! Ow! Eek!

Beatrice returns.

BEATRICE
Signore, I apologize! Sirrah! Fetch our dinner! Now!

Beatrice and Pantalone sit. Brighella exits to kitchen.

BEATRICE
I so thank you for dining with me, Signore.

PANTALONE
No, no. I thank you for dining with me!

BEATRICE
Not at all. After our misunderstanding I am most appreciative of your company. (awkward pause) (calls) Sirrah? Antipasta!

MUSIC: Finiculi, Finicula? (bouncy, gets faster throughout scene)

The following classic comic scene – the Dining Scene from Servant of Two Masters - is choreographed like a musical number with Truffaldino eventually bouncing like a pinball (SFX?) as the pace quickens. Shouts from offstage. Rhythmic banging of trays. Dishes appear from out of nowhere.

TRUFFALDINO (O.S.)
Antipasta, Maestro!

BRIGHELLA (O.S.)
Antipasta Brighella!

CHORUS (O.S.)
Antipasta Brighella!

Bang of trays. Truffaldino walks on with antipasta. Places it reverently.

TRUFFALDINO
Antipasta Brighella? Antipasta Brighella!

BEATRICE
Ah! You can bring the zuppa.

TRUFFALDINO
Si, Signore. I bring the zuppa. Subito!

TRUFFALDINO
Zuppa por favore, Maestro!

BRIGHELLA (O.S.)
Zuppa por favore!

CHORUS (O.S.)
Zuppa! Zuppa!

BRIGHELLA (O.S.)
Zuppa!

Bang of trays. Truffaldino enters quickly with soup.

TRUFFALDINO
Zuppa? Zuppa for Signore. Zuppa for Signore. Enjoy.

Truffaldino pulls out pepper cracker, grinds, takes antipasta, exits.

PANTALONE
I apologize my daughter cannot be in your presence until the ceremony, Signore Rasponi.

BEATRICE
I understand completely, Signore Pantalone. We value these traditions.

PANTALONE
Grazie, Signore Rasponi.

BEATRICE
I agree completely with your judgement, Signore.

PANTALONE
Grazie, Signore.

BEATRICE
And I applaud your consideration, Signore.

PANTALONE
I applaud your sensitivity to my situation, Signore.

BEATRICE
Friggin 'do, Truffaldino!

TRUFFALDINO
Friggin 'do, Signore! (heads off) Friggin'do, Maestro!

BRIGHELLA (O.S.)
Friggin 'do, cherubimo!

CHORUS (O.S.)
Friggin 'do! Friggin 'do!

Bang of trays. Truffaldino runs in with friggin'do.

TRUFFALDINO
Friggin'do? Here's your friggin 'do, Signore. (tosses soup dishes) Por Signore. Por Signore. Hot. Spicy. French.

Pepper again. Florindo enters.

FLORINDO
Where oh where is my beloved? I miss her so. It is so frustrating to have killed a man and not be able to tell someone.

Florindo sits at a table, back to Beatrice. Truffaldino enters with the roast platter and sauce.

FLORINDO
Aha! You there! Rigoletto!

TRUFFALDINO
Truffal-- uh oh.

FLORINDO
Truffluhoh, where are you going with that? Good! I'm starving.

TRUFFALDINO
Uh, it is...for you, Signore.

FLORINDO
For me?

TRUFFALDINO
I anticipate your every wish, Signore.

FLORINDO
As you should. Set it down. (he does) What is this?

TRUFFALDINO
Pig brains, excellency.

FLORINDO
You serve the roast first? Nonsense. Where is my antipasta? My zuppa?

TRUFFALDINO
Si, I'll get it, Signore. Excellent, Signore. Antipasta! Zuppa!

BRIGHELLA (O.S.)
Antipasta Brighella! Zuppa por Signori!

CHORUS (O.S.)
Antipasta Brighella! Zuppa!

Bang of trays. Truffaldino takes the roast and sauce to Beatrice's table.

TRUFFALDINO
Arritsotito, Signore.

BEATRICE
Well it's about time! What is it?

PANTALONE
Pig's ears. Just like Mama's. I mean, just like Mama makes.

TRUFFALDINO
(Pepper) Mangia bene. (Calling and dashing) Antipasta?

Obviously things are getting out of hand, out of sequence as in Mickey Mouse's "The Sorceror's Apprentice" sequence or Chaplin's "Modern Times". Improvisation and drill are key.

BRIGHELLA (O.S.)
Antipasta Brighella! Zuppa!

FLORINDO
(calling) Trumpalumpa?

TRUFFALDINO
Coming! Coming! Antipasta Brighella! Zuppa!

BRIGHELLA (O.S.)
Zuppa!

FLORINDO
It's about time!

TRUFFALDINO
Zuppa for maestro. Cracked pepper?

FLORINDO
Of course!

Truffaldino does pepper.

BEATRICE
Sirrah!

TRUFFALDINO
Si, Signore?

BEATRICE
The secundi?

TRUFFALDINO
Secundi now? Secundi with your primo?

BEATRICE
Si, now.

TRUFFALDINO
With the arristotiti?

BEATRICE
With the arrostitato.

TRUFFALDINO
Very well. Secundi!

BRIGHELLA (O.S.)
Secundi!

FLORINDO
I'm ready for my next...

TRUFFALDINO
Si, Signore!

Truffaldino takes the soup and exits.

BEATRICE
It's so hard to find good help, isn't it?

PANTALONE
Makes me long for bondage.

Truffaldino enters with plate for Florindo and plates for Beatrice.

TRUFFALDINO
Here's your friggin 'do.

FLORINDO
What's in it?

TRUFFALDINO
Kale and duckfat.

FLORINDO
Ah!

Truffaldino throws on pepper. Takes plate to Beatrice.

TRUFFALDINO
Secundi. Terzo. Beans with Spam. Beans with Spam. (pepper) Aha! (to audience) Did you hear a "grazie"?

Truffaldino exits, taking Florindo's plate.

FLORINDO
But I wasn't finished!

Truffaldino's gone mad. He exits, shoots right out again with roast, sauce, secundi, terzo for Florindo.

TRUFFALDINO
Primo, secundi, terzi for Signore!

FLORINDO
What's this? You bring them all at once?

TRUFFALDINO
You're not in Torino now, Signore! This is Venezia! Get on the gondola!

FLORINDO
But I --

Truffaldino goes to Beatrice's table.

PANTALONE
Another vino, when you have a moment?

Truffaldino looks daggers at him. Darts off again.

TRUFFALDINO
Una bodega de vino!

BRIGHELLA (O.S.)
Una bodega de vino!

CHORUS (O.S.)
Una bodega di vino!

He exits, comes back with bottle.

FLORINDO
Pepper, please! And a vino.

TRUFFALDINO
Una bodega de vino!

BRIGHELLA (O.S.)
Una bodega de vino!

BEATRICE
Truffaldino?

FLORINDO
Borsalino?

BEATRICE
Our dessert?

PANTALONE
Yes, what is the dessert?

TRUFFALDINO
A Trifle, Signore.

PANTALONE
What's a Trifle?

TRUFFALDINO
It's a limey pudding. A lumpy, bumpy, limey pudding.

FLORINDO
Boy? My dessert?

TRUFFALDINO
So, you want the trifle?

PANTALONE
Well--

BEATRICE
He tries. But after all, he is from Bergamo.

They chuckle.

FLORINDO
Waiter!

BRIGHELLA (O.S.)
Waiter!

CHORUS (O.S.)
Waiter!

PANTALONE
I'll try it.

Truffaldino starts to exit.

FLORINDO
What's for dessert, again?

TRUFFALDINO
Something new, Signore.

FLORINDO
What's it called?

TRUFFALDINO
A truffaldino! Truffaldino!

Truffaldino stalks off.

BRIGHELLA (O.S.)
Truffaldino! Truffaldino! Truffaldino!

CHORUS (O.S.)
Truffaldino! Truffaldino! Truffaldino!

FLORINDO
Truffalwhato?

Truffaldino stalks on, spitting into a huge gelatinous whipped cream pudding. He grabs a handful of it and plops it on Florindo's plate.

TRUFFALDINO
Truffaldino! Truffaldino! Truffaldino!

BRIGHELLA (O.S.)
Truffaldino! Truffaldino! Truffaldino!

CHORUS (O.S.)
Truffaldino! Truffaldino! Truffaldino!

Truffaldino walks over to Beatrice's and does same.

TRUFFALDINO
From Bergamo! Bergamo! Bergamo!

BRIGHELLA AND CHORUS (O.S.)
Truffaldino! Truffaldino! Truffaldino!

Truffaldino stalks off.

Pulls latch, sign flies down. "Closed!"

Blackout. Music.

SCENE 6

Smeraldina enters excitedly.

SMERALDINA
Such a mistress! I cannot believe Signora Clarice would send a girl of my innocence to a notorious hotel, where just anything might happen! Bongiorno, Signore...

BRIGHELLA
(wink) Bongiorno, Signora...

SMERALDINA
I have a letter here from my mistress to a "Signore Federigo Rasponi".

BRIGHELLA
Really? (teasing) Is that all you're here for?

SMERALDINA
Whatever do you mean, Signore?

BRIGHELLA
You're not just an angel sent to the Bohemian part of Venezia to torment me?

SMERALDINA
Bohemia? Is that where I am?!

BRIGHELLA
Why not. And this could be your lucky day. I am possibly in a position to introduce you to someone who might possibly be in a position to assist you.

Brighella winks and exits.

SMERALDINA
He seems to know a lot about positions.

BRIGHELLA (O.S.)
Hey, Bergamo! Some doll's lookin for ya!

SMERALDINA
Bergamo?!

Truffaldino enters eating a turkey leg.

TRUFFALDINO
Ciao, Signorina! (tosses turkey leg over backdrop)

SMERALDINA
I'm sorry to disturb you.

TRUFFALDINO
You're not disturbing me at all!

SMERALDINA
I have a letter for your master.

She starts to go.

TRUFFALDINO
Wait! You didn't give it to me. I'm glad you're here. I have a question.

SMERALDINA
A question?

TRUFFALDINO
Si. I have this friend. Who likes this person. And wonders if, perhaps, that person might be interested in, perhaps, meeting another person, who would be him, to see if that person might be interested in, perhaps, exploring a friendship in which a certain person, my friend, would be interested.

SMERALDINA
I'm sorry – what?

TRUFFALDINO
Well, if a certain person --

SMERALDINA
Tell your friend…I think it would be quite possible.

TRUFFALDINO
Really? I'll tell him!

SMERALDINA
Oh, this letter is for your master.

TRUFFALDINO
Really? What does it say?

SMERALDINA
I don't know. I know it's not a love letter.

TRUFFALDINO
Well if we don't know what's in it I'm not going to give it to him. He might kill the messenger. Let's see.

SMERALDINA
Be careful.

Truffaldino opens it.

TRUFFALDINO
Oops.

SMERALDINA
What have you done!

TRUFFALDINO
Don't worry, we have gum. What's it say?

SMERALDINA
I don't know. I can't read.

TRUFFALDINO
Neat! I can't either! I think that's an M.

SMERALDINA
No, that's a W.

They're looking opposite sides

TRUFFALDINO
Really?

SMERALDINA
Yeah. That's an W. See? Yours is upside down.

TRUFFALDINO
Oh yeah...

Beatrice and Pantalone enter.

BEATRICE
What's going on?

TRUFFALDINO
Gum! (Reaches under seat, chews, stamps gum on letter)

BEATRICE
Have you opened my letters again, sirrah?!

TRUFFALDINO
No, Signore! (offers the mangled letter)

BEATRICE
You have! Look at it!

TRUFFALDINO
You're right! It's awful! The postal service today has -- (to Smeraldina) Did you see this? (to audience) Did you?

BEATRICE
(reads) Signore, it is from Signora Clarice, warning of Silvio's insane jealousy.
(to Truffaldino) And you had the impudence to read this?

TRUFFALDINO
Of course not. I can't read!

PANTALONE
(to Smeraldina) Did you?

SMERALDINA
No, Signore!

BEATRICE
Well someone opened the letter…

TRUFFALDINO
Not me!

SMERALDINA
Not me!

BEATRICE
Who brought it?

SMERALDINA
Truffaldino.

TRUFFALDINO
Smeraldina.

BEATRICE
Who?

Truffaldino and Smeraldina immediately point to man in the audience.

BEATRICE
(to man) Is this true? No? And now you're lying! Are you with him, Madame? I pity you. Take care of him when you get home, eh?

PANTALONE
Smeraldina! You shall pay for your part in this. Come over here.

SMERALDINA
No.

PANTALONE
No? No? Then I'll come over there! Yaaaaah! (chases her off)

SMERALDINA
Noooooo!

BEATRICE
Sirrah! This is the second letter you've opened today! Is this the respect you show your master?

TRUFFALDINO
Signore, what can I say? I'm a servant. I never get a letter. If I see a letter, I have to open it. I'm just curious.

BEATRICE
Well I'm curious too. Do you like pizza?

TRUFFALDINO
Sure!

BEATRICE
Pepperoni?

Beatrice grabs a hanging "pepperoni" and beats him with it.

TRUFFALDINO
Ooh! Ah! Oh! Ah! Ow! Ooh!

Beatrice exits. Florindo enters.

FLORINDO
Trampoloony! What's going on here?

TRUFFALDINO
I have no idea, Signore. I was just standing here. That man went nuts on me.

FLORINDO
You let him do that to me?

TRUFFALDINO
To you?

FLORINDO
Of course! An attack on my servant is an attack on me! I can understand you not defending yourself, because you are worthless, but to not defend me is a double insult! You say you are a vegetarian! Therefore I spare you the pepperoni.

TRUFFALDINO
Oh thank you, Signore.

FLORINDO
I give you the zuchinni!

Florindo grabs a hanging "zuchinni" and beats Truffaldino.

TRUFFALDINO
Ooh! Ah! Oh! Ah! Ow!

Florindo exits.

TRUFFALDINO
You could just fire me, y'know!

He starts to clean up. Blackout.

At this awkward moment a member of the cast steps forward to sing an aria badly. Obviously to cover the scene change until Truffaldino is ready.

SCENE 7

Truffaldino enters cheerfully with two trunks. Hangs out clothes from both, and sprays Fabrezio while speaking to the audience.

TRUFFALDINO
Both my masters are sleeping. Now is my chance to get a little work done. One of the most important jobs of a servant in the 18th Century is that of the "personal valet". That means that I am in charge of making sure my master's clothes are fresh and ready for wear, so as not to "offend". In the 18th Century a stylish master should never be a stinky master!

Florindo enters.

FLORINDO
Turtlino, what are you dering?

TRUFFALDINO
I'm airing out your clothing, Signore!

FLORINDO
Excellent. Aha! What are these clerthes over here?

TRUFFALDINO
Oh. Uh -- I do not know, Signore.

FLORINDO
Well hand me my black coat. I will wear it this evening.

TRUFFALDINO
The black coat. (to audience) Yikes. Which black coat is his? Eeny meeny miny... This one? Wish me luck.

Truffaldino hands Florindo the coat.

FLORINDO
Very good. Wait! What's this? Something in the pocket? A pertrait...of Beatrice! Azusa! Zamboni, where did this pertrait come from?

TRUFFALDINO
What, Signore? Oh that portrait. Well, yes. Please forgive me, Signore. It belongs to me. I put it in the coat. For safe-keeping.

FLORINDO
But whir did you get it? Quickly!

TRUFFALDINO
(near tears) From -- my master. Another master. Who died. And left me this.

FLORINDO
Died? No! And when did this mester die?

TRUFFALDINO
A week ago. (aside) Pretty quick, huh?

FLORINDO
And what was your mester's nim?

TRUFFALDINO
His – he never told me. We didn't know each other all that well.

FLORINDO
(Aside) I fir his mester was my Beatrice! She fled Torino at about that time, in min's clothing. (to him) Tell me, was he -- young?

TRUFFALDINO
Si, he was -- young.

FLORINDO
And did he have a bird?

TRUFFALDINO
A bird? No, he never did. He wanted one, but --

FLORINDO
No, no, a bird. On his cheen.

TRUFFALDINO
His cheen? I -- Oh a beard! Ye--no... (aside) This is fun.

FLORINDO
And was he from -- Torino?

TRUFFALDINO
From Torino. Sure.

FLORINDO
And he is merto?

TRUFFALDINO
Morto.

FLORINDO
How?

TRUFFALDINO
He was -- trampled by a herd of rabid -- goats. Sheep.

FLORINDO
Oh! And where was he bird?

TRUFFALDINO
Bird again. Where was he -- oh buried! Well. Tough one. He was buried...he wasn't buried. What was left of him, after the goats, was put into an urn, and taken to Torino by his servant.

FLORINDO
And was this the sim servant who...!

TRUFFALDINO
Si! Pasquale! You remembered, Signore! I'll tell him. He'll be very...

FLORINDO
(Aside) These words are deggers to my soul. Oh my Beatrice! Your longing for me has killed you! Oh! Oh! Beatrice!

Florindo staggers off.

TRUFFALDINO
Wow. He must have known the guy.

Beatrice enters with Pantalone.

BEATRICE
But there are still costs unaccounted for, Signor Pantalone.

PANTALONE
Well I will go over my list, Signore Federigo, and take care of it.

BEATRICE
I brought my own; so we can match lists, eh? You there, Truffaldino! What are these clothes doing here?

TRUFFALDINO
I'm airing them, Signore.

BEATRICE
Good. Go to my trunk and hand me my book of accounts.

TRUFFALDINO
Si, Signore.

Truffaldino goes to Florindo's trunk and hands a book to Beatrice.

BEATRICE
(Aside) What's this?! The letters I sent to Florindo! Where did you get this book?

TRUFFALDINO
Uh, it's mine, Signore. I put it in your trunk to keep it safe.

BEATRICE
But where did you get it?

TRUFFALDINO
My master gave it to me.

BEATRICE
Your master?

TRUFFALDINO
The one before you. He gave it to me...and then he was killed...and I kept it.

BEATRICE
Killed?! He was killed?! How?

TRUFFALDINO
He was hit by -- a runaway cart of -- fettucini.

BEATRICE
How awful!

TRUFFALDINO
How awful? Pretty awful. It was a mess.

BEATRICE
And was his name...Florindo?

TRUFFALDINO
(aside) Sure. (aloud) Florindo!

BEATRICE
And his last name...Aretusi?

TRUFFALDINO
Gezundheit. Oh, sorry. Aretusi, si.

BEATRICE
Oh Florindo! Mi amore! Morto? All hope is lost. Fate is so fickle. I leave Torino. I dress as a man. Si, sirrah, I am a woman. I risk my life to come to Venezia, only to find my love is dead? Why do women bother?! Now, my love, I follow you. Follow you -- to my tomb!

Beatrice exits, arms outstretched, like Judith Anderson in "Medea".

PANTALONE
A w-woman? He's a woman? Why would he be a woman?

TRUFFALDINO
My master is a mistress? Mama mia, this must be Venezia.

Truffaldino exits.

PANTALONE
Why would he do that? Be a woman? The plays of this period are silly but that's -- don't you think?

SCENE 8

Silvio enters.

PANTALONE
Silvio, my boy! I am suddenly delighted to see you!

Pantalone gives Silvio a big hug, checking out his masculinity.

SILVIO
Signore! Thank you for that warm greeting. (pulls dagger) But now --

PANTALONE
Wait, my boy! Put that away! I've thought it over, remembering the nights of romance that passed between Signora Pantalone and me, before the accident, God rest her soul. I've realized love is so much more important than property. (sotto) You still have your inheritance, don't you?

SILVIO
Si, but--

PANTALONE
It's settled then! Clarice shall be yours!

SILVIO
Signore Pantalone! Can this be? Am I worthy?

PANTALONE
It can! You are! We'll put the deal together immediately.

SILVIO
This makes me so happy…Papa! Please forgive my temper before.

PANTALONE
Of course.

SILVIO
When I said I'd "do you in" I didn't mean it.

PANTALONE
Of course not.

SILVIO
When I said I'd "rip your head off", it was a figure of speech.

PANTALONE
Of course. And when I called you "dumb as a stump"-- Let's find Clarice.

They exit.

SCENE 9

Tragic music. Puccini? Adele? Isolated on either side of the stage, Beatrice and Florindo slowly enter holding rubber daggers. Beatrice has the book. Florindo has the portrait. Their moves are synchronized. They raise the daggers to their chests, reconsider, then raise them again. At climactic moment they call out.

FLORINDO
Beatrice!

BEATRICE
Florindo!

They turn and see each other.

FLORINDO
Stip!

BEATRICE
Stop!

FLORINDO
My belowéd!

BEATRICE
Mi amore!

They run to each other and embrace, madly kissing. Start to tango.

FLORINDO
Oh my darling! You were gong to keel yourself? Why would you think of doing sich a ting?

BEATRICE
Because I had lost you, my darling.

FLORINDO
I thought you were dead!

BEATRICE
And I you.

FLORINDO
What?

BEATRICE
Me too.

FLORINDO
Who told you I was did?

BEATRICE
My servant. He gave me this book.

FLORINDO
But it was in my trink. How did it get to you? Aha! Perhaps the very same way your pertrait cim to me!

BEATRICE
Our servants!

FLORINDO
We must find them!

Truffaldino enters.

BEATRICE
You! Come here at once! Don't be frightened.

TRUFFALDINO
(aside) Caught. Caught like a rat in a trap!

Truffaldino goes to them.

FLORINDO
So, liddle minkey, perhaps you can esplain yourself!

TRUFFALDINO
Oh I wish I could, Signore. My own mother doesn't understand me.

FLORINDO
How did the pertrait and book come to be in the tronks! And how did your little compenion in crime assist you!

TRUFFALDINO
(Aside) That's it! (aloud) Shhhh, Signore! (sotto to Florindo) I must speak to you alone, Signore, of things only a man would understand.

He pulls Florindo aside.

FLORINDO
Well?

TRUFFALDINO
Signore, all this mischief has been the work of my friend Pasquale.

FLORINDO
Pasquale? You mean--

TRUFFALDINO
The Signora's servant. Pasquale is the boob who mixed up the coats and the portrait and the books. And then he begged me to cover for him.

FLORINDO
But why did you?

TRUFFALDINO
What can I say, Signore? He too is from Bergamo. In Bergamo we have a saying, "Vente macchiato!"

FLORINDO
But that -- that means nothing.

TRUFFALDINO
To you. You are not a Bergamesi. I could not let him down. Or there would be...repercussions...

FLORINDO
Ah! The Sinatras?

TRUFFALDINO
I say nothing.

BEATRICE
What's taking so long over there?

They rejoin Beatrice.

FLORINDO
He was just telling me --

TRUFFALDINO
Signore! If I may speak with you, Signora?

He pulls her aside.

BEATRICE
What have you been telling him?

TRUFFALDINO
If you must know, Signora. Signore has in his service a most unscrupulous rascal named Pasquale. He has caused this mess. But I just told the Signore that it was my fault.

BEATRICE
But why?

TRUFFALDINO
For the love I bear my Pasquale!

BEATRICE
Oh. How do you know this -- Pasquale?

TRUFFALDINO
We were boys together in Bergamo. He pulled me from a stopped up sewer when I was five. He called me "little chunks". We've gone our separate ways, but I still owe him my life. So I beg you! Do not let Signore know the truth.

BEATRICE
Very well. But you both should be ashamed.

FLORINDO
Now, my dir, in honor of our newfound heppiness let us be chiritable.

Truffaldino shares winks with both.

BEATRICE
But come, I must see Signore Pantalone. Will you join me?

FLORINDO
First I must see a benker. I will be with you shirely.

BEATRICE
With Shirley? Oh. Till then, my love.

They kiss.

TRUFFALDINO
(sotto to Florindo) Signore, perhaps I should assist the Signora.

FLORINDO
Good idea. Take ker of her.

TRUFFALDINO
And, Signore, might I ask a favor?

FLORINDO
Fervors? You are asking fervors?

TRUFFALDINO
A little one. At Signore Pantalone's, there is a beautiful servant whom I believe could possibly, one day make me as happy as the beautiful Signora makes you. Perhaps you could mention it?

FLORINDO
I understand, little servant man. Well, we shall see.

They exit.

SCENE 10

Clarice in tears, with Pantalone, Lombardi, Brighella, Silvio, Smeraldina.

SILVIO
Aw come on, Clarice. Marry me.

PANTALONE
You know he loves you.

SMERALDINA
Oh for heaven's sakes. Signora! He loves you. And you love him most of the time. So do as most women do. Bite the bullet and marry him.

CLARICE
But to distrust me...

SILVIO
Aw, Clarice...

CLARICE
To accuse me of cheating...

SILVIO
I'm a shmozo. But I'll never distrust you again. And you can bring this up whenever we argue.

CLARICE
Oh all right. You wore me down.

SMERALDINA
This is so romantic!

Silvio and Clarice embrace. Big cheer from everywhere.

Beatrice and Florindo enter.

BEATRICE
Buona giornata, mi amici!

PANTALONE
Signor Federigo! I mean--

CLARICE
Signora Beatrice, Papa!

PANTALONE
It's the pants.

BEATRICE
I beg your forgiveness, Clarice, for causing such distress to your family.

CLARICE
Not at all. You were the most exciting part. This may be the last excitement I'll ever have! You'll be in my wedding, of course?

BEATRICE
Of course! Oh I feel better. You are so—lucky.

They embrace.

FLORINDO
Ahim...

BEATRICE
But I now want you all to meet my betrothed -- Signor Florindo Aretusi.

SMERALDINA
Oh my!

FLORINDO
My frinds, I am delitted ah wull finnally expiryence the ability to enjoy the hospitility fr which Venezia is so will reputationed.

Beat while everyone figures out what he said.

PANTALONE
Yes, well we're glad to have you, Signore. (All cheer) It looks like a double wedding! We'll split the cost, hey? So now --

TRUFFALDINO
Wait! Scusi! Signore Florindo! About my request? The fervor?

FLORINDO
Ah! Of curse. Signore Pantalone, my servant has apperently become smitened with yr daughter's serving mid. And he has esked me if I may be so bild, as to requist permission to sik her hind in mitrimony.

PANTALONE
I caught so little of that. What did he say?

CLARICE
The little fellow wants...Oh, Signore, I'm so sorry. But I've already promised Smeraldina's hand to Pasquale, the servant of Signora Beatrice.

FLORINDO
My little frind, I know you are hurtbroken. But if she is already promised to yur Pasquale, Signora --

BEATRICE
No, Florindo. Not to my Pasquale. Your Pasquale.

FLORINDO
No, yur Pasquale.

BEATRICE
I don't have a Pasquale.

FLORINDO
And I din't have a Pasquale. Thin who has a Pasquale? (to audience) Do eny of you have a Pasquale? You, sir?

Everyone questions everyone, denying Pasquales.

TRUFFALDINO
Tutti! Hold everything! Come here at once, mi bella donna!

Truffaldino sweeps Smeraldina to center.

Signora Smeraldina di Venezia, do you agree to marry, as you must out of loyalty to your mistress, the servant of Signora Beatrice of Torino?

SMERALDINA
I guess…I must.

TRUFFALDINO
And you give your consent?

CLARICE
I must.

TRUFFALDINO
And yet, you would also agree to marry the servant of Signor Florindo of Torino?

SMERALDINA
With all my heart.

TRUFFALDINO
And you give your consent?

FLORINDO
Of curse I der.

TRUFFALDINO
And "I der ter"! For now you and all the world should know… that I myself am both Pasquale Rossetti di Parmagiani di Bergamo and Truffaldino Battachio Boyardee de Bergamo! And, with the love of this, the most beautiful lady in all of Italy, I am the happiest man in all Venezia!

ALL
Yaaaaaaaay!

MUSIC: Wedding march. Everyone pairs up and exits.

Brighella happily hosts.

FINALE

Printed in Great Britain
by Amazon